WA7

Please renew or return items by the date shown on your receipt

www.hertsdirect.org/libraries

Renewals and enquiries: 0300 123 4049

Textphone for hearing or speech impaired   0300 123 4041

Hertfordshire

in accordance with the Copyright, Designs and Patents Act, 1988.
A CIP catalogue record for this book is available from the British Library.
ISBN 1 84121 414 0
9 10 8
Printed in China

D0280892

★ The Fried Piper ★ Shampoozel ★ Daft Jack ★ The Emperor ★
★ Little Red Riding Wolf ★ Rumply Crumply Stinky Pin ★

☆ Ghostyshocks ☆ Snow White ☆ Cinderboy ☆ Eco-Wolf ☆
☆ The Greedy Farmer ☆ Billy Beast ☆

Round about lunch time, the greedy farmer began to feel hungry. His huge belly rumbled as he walked across the field.

Suddenly, he noticed a rather small turnip. . .

. . . but it was far too small for his lunch.

The farmer called over to his wife.

"Here you are, wife," he said, "you can
have this nice turnip for your lunch."

The farmer's wife looked at the rather small turnip. She poked it with her boot.

"You mean old thing!" she said to her
husband, "I won't get very fat on that!"

So the farmer's wife called the cow.

The cow looked at the turnip.

She poked it with her hoof.

"There you are," said the farmer and the farmer's wife, "we're feeling generous today. You can have this delicious turnip all for yourself."

"You must be joking," mooed the cow, "that's not enough for a big girl like me. Call the goat."

The goat looked at the rather small turnip.

He prodded it with his horn.

21

"We have chosen this beautiful turnip especially for you," said the farmer and the farmer's wife and the cow. "Would you like to eat it here or take it away?"

"You must be kidding," bleated the goat. "I've never seen such a lousy specimen. Give it to the dog."

The dog sniffed the turnip.

"Go on," said the farmer, his wife, the cow and the goat. "Tuck in."

"Don't make me laugh," barked the dog.
"I don't even like turnip. Call the cat."

The cat came. . . slowly.

"Guess what?" said the farmer, the farmer's wife, the cow, the goat and the dog. "It's your lucky day. You can have this turnip boiled, mashed, poached or steamed – all garnished with side salad and served with house wine."

"Humph!" miaowed the cat, looking at the turnip. "I've got bigger blisters than this turnip. Send for the mouse."

The mouse scampered across the field.

She came to the place where the farmer,
the farmer's wife, the cow, the goat, the
dog and the cat were standing.

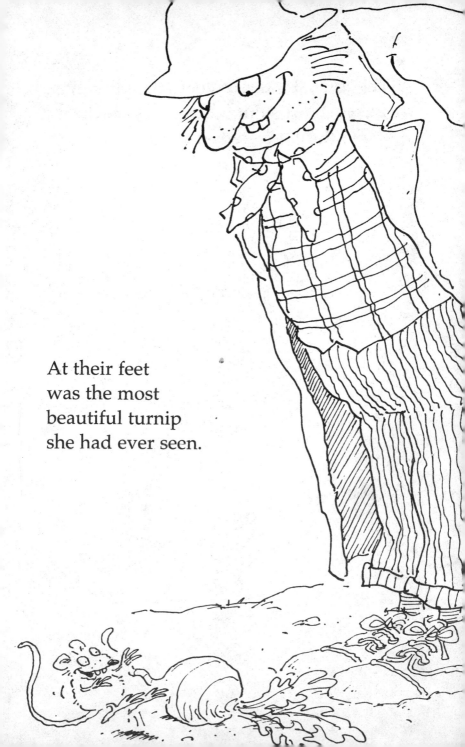

At their feet
was the most
beautiful turnip
she had ever seen.

The mouse stared and her pink nose twitched. She couldn't believe her luck. She LOVED turnips.

She sniffed it. She licked it all over and her eyes sparkled.

"Don't wait for us," said the farmer, the farmer's wife, the cow, the goat, the dog and the cat.

41

So the tiny mouse began to eat. She
nibbled and gnawed.

It took a long time because, to her it was
a very BIG turnip.

The others watched and waited and felt
more and more hungry. The greedy farmer's
belly rumbled.

The mouse crunched. . .

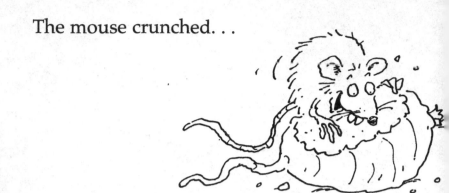

. . . and scrunched.

And chewed. . .

. . . and chomped.

Until, at last, every scrap of the rather
small turnip was gone.

Then the tiny mouse burped a tiny burp, sighed a tiny sigh, rubbed her tiny fat mousy tummy. . .

. . . and lay down in the grass for a tiny
mousy sleep.

The cat looked at the fat little mouse.

"Now, that's what I call LUNCH!" she growled. And she gobbled up the little mouse in one bite.

Then. . . the cat was eaten by the dog. . .

. . . the dog was eaten by the goat . . .

. . . the goat was eaten by the cow . . .

. . . the cow was eaten by the farmer's wife . . .

. . . and the farmer's wife was eaten by. . .

"WAIT A MINUTE!" shouted the farmer's wife, "You can't eat ME!"

"But what about my lunch," moaned the greedy farmer.

"Well," said the farmer's wife, patting her tummy. "You should have eaten that turnip. It was absolutely delicious!"